Verity Fairy
AND
Cinderella

Written by Caroline Wakeman
Illustrated by Amy Zhing

Contents

Fairy Tale Kingdom

Sleeping Beauty's Castle

Clock Tower

Celeste's House

Verity's House

Wicked Queen's Castle

Chapter One
A Midsummer Night

It was a very special night in the Fairy Tale Kingdom. The fairies were celebrating the longest day of the year. They all gathered around the clock tower. Each fairy held a bright, flickering candle. They waited eagerly for the clock to strike twelve.

Verity and Celeste stood next to each other. Their faces were bathed in the glow of the candlelight. They were both beaming with excitement.

"This is my favorite night of the year!" Verity said eagerly. She bounced up and down on her toes.

"It's so much fun to stay up late!" Celeste agreed. She carefully held her candleholder with both hands.

The two fairies were the best of friends and loved spending time together. They liked making fairy cakes, playing games, and reading their favorite magazine, *Sparkle Time*.

"There's only one ceremony I like more," Verity said knowingly.

Celeste chuckled. She knew exactly which ceremony Verity was talking about.

The fairies worked hard to keep everyone happy and safe in the Fairy Tale Kingdom. At each full moon, they all gathered around the enchanted tree. Tatiana, the Queen of the Fairies, would announce which fairy had worked the hardest. The lucky fairy was presented with a beautiful sparkly star.

Celeste also knew that Verity really wanted to be the first fairy to have the rare lilac star. It was all Verity could talk about.

The first **chime** of the bell struck and all the fairies looked up at the clock. They counted all twelve chimes together and blew out their candles on the twelfth strike. There was a moment of silence as they each made their wish. A loud cheer then rippled through the village.

chime   Ringing sound

"What did you wish for?" Verity asked
Celeste.

"You're not supposed to say what you
wished for or it won't come—"

"Marshmallows!" Verity shouted before
Celeste could finish. "I wished for lots and

lots of marshmallows!" Verity licked her lips.

As the excitement died down, Verity could see Tatiana making her way toward her. Verity crossed her fingers. She really wanted Tatiana to give her an important job so she could earn another sparkly star.

"Hello, Verity," said Tatiana as she sat down next to her. "I have a job for you. Please can you help the Fairy Godmother?

I'm afraid she keeps forgetting things."

"I don't usually forget things," Verity replied confidently. "Hold on... did I blow my candle out? Oh yes, I did, when I made a wish—phew!"

Tatiana smiled and then quickly looked serious. "The Fairy Godmother needs to make sure that Cinderella gets to the prince's ball. Poor Cinderella works so hard for her stepsisters." Tatiana shook her head sadly. "They treat her very badly!"

"I could make the Fairy Godmother a list of things she needs to do to remind her. I'm very good at lists," Verity said proudly.

"Great idea," said Tatiana. "Making lists is an excellent way to help the Fairy Godmother stay **organized**."

organized   Kept in good order

Then Tatiana yawned. "I think we should all go to bed now. You just need to make sure you're at the Fairy Godmother's house tomorrow night by seven thirty. Cinderella must be at the prince's ball by eight thirty. That's when the castle doors close, so she can't be late. Good luck, Verity."

Verity waved goodbye to Tatiana and then sat back down. She put her head in her hands. There was one HUGE problem— Verity didn't know how to tell time! She didn't want anyone to know, not even Celeste. But how could Verity help Cinderella if she couldn't make sure she was at the ball before the doors closed?

Chapter Two
Verity Pays a Visit

The next evening, Verity finished her dinner as quickly as she could. She had decided to fly straight to the Fairy Godmother's house. She was determined not to be late.

Verity **fluttered** down to a pretty brick house. White flowers climbed up at the front and twisted around the red front door. She could hear the TV blaring from the open

fluttered   Flew quickly and lightly

windows. The lace curtains flapped in the gentle breeze. The sweet smell of honeysuckle filled the air. Verity entered the open front door. There were piles of letters and newspapers all over the hall floor. She found the Fairy Godmother sitting in her lounge watching TV.

"I'm Verity. Tatiana, Queen of the Fairies, sent me to help you. I'm a fairy, by the way." Verity showed the Fairy Godmother her wand as **proof**.

"That's nice, dear," said the Fairy Godmother without looking away from the TV.

"What can I do to help?" Verity noticed that the lounge was even messier than the hall.

"Shh," replied the Fairy Godmother. "Flora is about to find out that Fauna has been saying nasty things about her."

Verity rolled her eyes—she had seen this show before and didn't like it. "I'll make you a nice cup of milk and honey," said Verity.

proof Evidence to show something is true

There were piles of dirty plates and dishes everywhere in the kitchen, even on the floor! Verity set to work and the kitchen was soon spotless. She gave the Fairy Godmother her drink just as the programme ended.

"Thank you, dear." The Fairy
Godmother seemed happy to see her now.
"What am I supposed to be doing today? I
wrote it down somewhere." She looked
around and then glanced at her watch. "Oh,
here it is, on the back of my hand!"

Verity hid a smile. Tatiana was right—
the Fairy Godmother seemed to forget
everything!

"Today I need to..." the
Fairy Godmother
squinted to read her
writing. "Oh, where
are my glasses?"
She looked under a
huge pile of
magazines.

"They're on your head." Verity pointed.

The Fairy Godmother patted the top of her head. "So, they are! I wonder who put them there?" she giggled. "Cinderella. Ball. 8:30pm!" she read. "If only I could remember what that meant?"

"Maybe it means you need to get Cinderella to the prince's ball by eight thirty?" Verity suggested.

"I think you're right, dear. We'd better go!" The Fairy Godmother grabbed her bag. She checked she was still wearing her glasses, and they both flew to Cinderella's house.

*

Verity and the Fairy Godmother waited outside Cinderella's house. The stepsisters were getting ready to leave for the prince's ball. Verity noticed how extremely neat and tidy everything was.

Verity flew up to a window to peek inside and almost banged her head. The glass was so clean that she thought it was open! She could see Cinderella adjusting the skirt of the eldest stepsister's beautiful rose-colored ballgown.

"Oh," exclaimed Cinderella. "I wish that one day I could have a dress as beautiful as yours!"

The two sisters shrieked with laughter. "YOU? Why would you need a beautiful dress? All you ever do is clean."

"And it doesn't really go with rainbow slippers!" Both the stepsisters cackled loudly.

Cinderella looked down sadly at her colorful slippers. "What's wrong with them? I love my slippers!" she whispered softly.

Moments later, the two stepsisters ran out of the house. They **clambered** into the horse and carriage that was waiting to take them to the prince's castle.

---

clambered   Climbed

The Fairy Godmother frowned. "They're so mean. But, I have a plan that will change Cinderella's life forever!"

Verity listened eagerly as the Fairy Godmother explained. She wrote down a list in her notepad of all the things they needed to do.

They found Cinderella in the house cleaning up after her stepsisters.

"You shall go to the ball!" announced the Fairy Godmother.

Chapter Three
Cinderella's Slippers

Verity quickly introduced herself to Cinderella, who was looking very surprised.

"I'm Verity. I've been sent by Tatiana, Queen of the Fairies, to help the Fairy Godmother. She's very busy, you know. I'm a fairy, by the way." Verity showed Cinderella her wand as proof.

"Umm... hello," said Cinderella. Her dress

was made of dull-colored patches sewn together and her hair was messy.

Verity looked at Cinderella's feet and smiled. "I like your slippers. Rainbow-color is my favorite! But I think you might need to wear something a little fancier for the prince's party." Verity gently nudged the Fairy Godmother who was digging through her bag.

"Oh, that's right." The Fairy Godmother **frantically** started looking around.

"Have you lost something?" Verity asked the Fairy Godmother.

"No need to panic, dear, but I seem to have lost my wand!"

Verity dropped her head in her hands. This task was not going to be easy.

*

After a long search, Verity let out a deep sigh.

The Fairy Godmother scratched her head as she tried to remember where she had last seen her wand. "Ha! It's in my hair!" she cried. "You must think I'm very forgetful!"

Verity knew now wasn't the time to tell the truth. She smiled and shook her head.

frantically   Wildly and uncontrollably

Besides, she often did the same thing.

The Fairy Godmother quickly waved her wand and Cinderella was ready to go to the ball.

Verity was amazed at how different Cinderella looked. Her hair was elegantly styled. Her blue eyes sparkled with delight. Most importantly—she looked happy.

"Wow! This is the most beautiful dress I've ever seen." Cinderella beamed as she looked down at the dazzling jade-green dress that had a full-length skirt decorated with **diamante**.

"I'll check my list to make sure we haven't forgotten anything," said Verity. "Beautiful dress and tiara—check. Pumpkin-style coach —check. Six footmen and a driver—check. Glass slippers?"

Cinderella was still wearing her rainbow slippers.

"You can't wear those! This is THE party of the year!"

"I like these slippers," said Cinderella. "They're really comfortable, and they make me happy."

diamante   Tiny disks that sparkle like diamonds

The Fairy Godmother shook her head. "Oh no dear, the prince won't be impressed," she said. "And he must fall madly in love with you, so you can both live happily ever after!"

Chapter Four
The Prince's Ball

The Fairy Godmother waved her wand again. A beautiful pair of glass slippers appeared on Cinderella's feet. Then to Verity's surprise, the Fairy Godmother made herself comfortable on the sofa with a book.

"Shouldn't we go now?" Verity asked.

The Fairy Godmother checked her watch. "You should hurry up, dear. Time is passing fast—you don't want to be late!"

"Are you not coming?" Verity frowned.

"Oh no, dear, I can't miss this show."
The Fairy Godmother put her book down
then pointed the remote at the TV and
pulled out a bag of mints.

Verity was shocked. "But there are so
many other more interesting things you
could be doing. Like judo. Or waterskiing.
Or, I don't know, going to the biggest party
of the year!"

But the Fairy Godmother didn't seem to
be listening. "Don't forget to be back by
midnight," she said casually.

"Excuse me?" Verity said slowly.

"Well, if you don't leave the ball by
midnight then Cinderella's dress will turn

back into rags. Her coach will turn into a pumpkin and the footmen and driver will become mice and rats! Now off you go, dear. Have fun, and I'll see you tomorrow." She waved Verity away.

"Oh, pickled pumpkins!" sighed Verity as she took Cinderella to the carriage waiting outside the house.

"No, it's just a normal pumpkin, dear!" the Fairy Godmother shouted after her. She shook her head. "I wouldn't use pickled pumpkins as a coach... it would smell like vinegar!"

The inside of the coach was very **luxurious**. Everything was made of velvet and the seats were extremely comfortable. But Verity was too worried to enjoy the ride. She had no idea how she would know when it was midnight!

*

The prince's castle was beautiful. Cinderella and Verity entered through the huge wooden doors, which quickly slammed shut behind them. Verity wiped her forehead with relief—they had arrived just in time.

---

luxurious Very comfortable and expensive

There was an enormous banquet spread across heaving tables. Verity spotted marshmallows and a chocolate fountain. Her two favorite foods! She would definitely be helping herself to those later.

Everybody stared at Cinderella. Verity felt very proud. She could see that the prince was just behind Cinderella, but she needed to come up with a way for him to notice her.

"Can I take your picture?" Verity asked Cinderella. "I want to enter the competition in this week's *Sparkle Time*."

"Ooh yes, I've never had my picture taken before." Cinderella was very excited.

Verity grabbed her camera from her backpack and looked through the lens. "Move back," she told Cinderella. "Back a bit more... keep going."

As Cinderella moved backward, she stumbled into the prince. They both giggled and within seconds they were dancing together. Verity was thrilled that her plan had worked.

A crowd had formed a circle around the couple as they danced. Verity spotted the seven dwarfs helping themselves to the food. She smiled to herself—they never missed a good party! She moved nearer to the dancers and found herself next to the two stepsisters.

"She looks very familiar!" one of the sisters said to the other. "Is she famous?"

Verity held her breath. If the stepsisters realized it was Cinderella, then they could wreck everything.

Chapter Five

What Time is it?

Quickly, Verity flew in front of the mean sisters. "Excuse me, can you tell me the time, please?" she asked sweetly.

"Move out of the way, you annoying little fairy," snapped one of the sisters rudely.

"Did you know there are two princes in the garden, looking for two **glamorous** sisters to dance with," Verity told them.

"Where? Where?" the sisters demanded.

"By the pond," Verity replied confidently. The stepsisters ran out to the garden as fast as they could.

Verity smiled as she watched Cinderella dancing with the prince, lost in happiness. Cinderella looked as though she could dance all night, but Verity knew they had to be careful. How much time had gone by? It would be terrible if the prince saw Cinderella in her rags and rainbow slippers.

*

Outside, Celeste could see her friend looking puzzled. She quickly flew in through the window and offered Verity a marshmallow.

"Celeste!" exclaimed Verity. "What are you doing here?"

"This is such a great party!" said Celeste happily.

"Wait a minute," said Verity **suspiciously**. "Were you invited by the prince?"

"I came to see you!" said Celeste.

"Umm, that's very naughty!" Verity said dramatically.

Celeste rolled her eyes. "I thought you might need some help?"

"Well... maybe..." Verity twiddled with her pink hair nervously. "The Fairy Godmother has left me in charge and Cinderella needs to leave by midnight."

"So, do you need some help?" Celeste asked encouragingly.

suspiciously   With a feeling that someone is behaving badly

A single tear rolled down Verity's cheek.

"I can't tell the time," she whispered. "You probably think I'm really silly."

Celeste put her arm around Verity. "I don't think that at all. You should have told me," Celeste said kindly. "You're my best friend. I would help you with anything and I would never think you were silly!"

"Thank you, Celeste." Verity gave Celeste a big hug.

"So, what time is it now?" Celeste asked Verity.

"I don't own a watch!" Verity thought this was obvious. Why would she wear a watch if she couldn't tell time? "What does your watch say?"

"I'm not wearing one," Celeste told Verity.

"Uh-oh," said Verity quietly. "How will we know when it's midnight?"

Chapter Six
Midnight Strikes

Celeste and Verity flew around the room looking everywhere for a clock.

"This is **disastrous**!" exclaimed Celeste.

Verity frowned. "I don't have time to try and figure out what your long word means—is that good or bad?"

"Bad!" Celeste groaned.

Just then, loud chimes started to ring

disastrous   Bad consequences and effects

from the large clock in the reception hall. As Verity counted the chimes, it reminded her of standing with her candle at the longest-day ceremony. Suddenly she realized something. "Celeste, is midnight the same time as twelve o'clock?"

"Yes!" Celeste flew over to one of the seven dwarfs, who was fast asleep on a chair. She checked the time on his watch. "Verity," she cried, "it's about to turn midnight! You need to get Cinderella home before the last chime!"

Quick as a flash, Verity pulled Cinderella
out of the castle. As they ran down the steps,
the coach turned into a pumpkin,
Cinderella's dress turned into rags and her
hair became messy.

"Stop!" shouted Cinderella as she took both glass shoes off her feet. "I can't run in these."

Verity quickly took her by the arm, eager to get her away from the palace before the prince saw them, but one of the shoes fell out of Cinderella's hand.

"Oh no!" exclaimed Verity.

"Don't worry," replied Cinderella. "I won't wear them again."

They arrived back at Cinderella's house just before her stepsisters. Verity quickly hid behind the curtains. Cinderella was sweeping the floor as the two sisters fell through the front door. They were both completely soaked.

"Oh my goodness!" exclaimed Cinderella. "What happened?"

"A funny little fairy told us that two princes were waiting by the pond in the garden for two sisters to dance with them," said one of the sisters. She dried her dripping hair with a towel. "But we waited for ages and then suddenly a frog jumped up onto my shoulder. I was so startled that I fell backward into the pond."

"Taking me with you!" shouted the second sister, angrily.

Verity giggled quietly as the mean sisters stomped upstairs to bed.

*

The next morning there was a loud knock at the door which startled Verity. She tried to wake Cinderella but she was fast asleep, smiling happily and dreaming of her night at the ball.

One of the stepsisters opened the door. "Oh my, it's the prince!" she shrieked and fluttered her eyelashes. "Have you come to see me?"

The prince stepped inside. "I'm here to find the owner of this beautiful glass slipper. I will marry the person whose foot fits this shoe!"

"Pickled pumpkins!" gasped Verity. She shook Cinderella by the shoulder. "Wake up! The prince is here with your slipper!"

Cinderella rubbed her eyes and looked at her feet. "It's OK—I've got both my slippers!" She yawned.

"I don't mean your rainbow slippers." Verity shook her head. "I mean the glass shoe that you lost at the ball last night! You need to show the prince it fits your foot."

They both crept quietly over to the bannisters and watched as the stepsisters tried to fit their huge feet into Cinderella's **dainty** glass slipper.

The prince slumped down on the chair and held his head in his hands. "I just want to find the person I met last night! She was

dainty   Small and delicate

great. We talked about all kinds of things and she was really fun to be with. Oh, I wish I could find her!"

Cinderella smiled at Verity and gently squeezed her hand. She then tiptoed over to the prince and tapped him lightly on the shoulder. "May I try the glass slipper on?"

The prince looked up at Cinderella and knew immediately she was the person he had been looking for. His face lit up in delight. "There's no need," he replied. "I'm so glad I found you." He looked down at Cinderella's feet. "I like your rainbow-colored slippers!" They both smiled.

Verity punched the air for joy. She was very happy for Cinderella.

Chapter Seven
Verity's Slippers

Later that day, Verity visited the Fairy
Godmother. Verity told her in great detail
what had happened at the party. She
described how the prince had searched for
Cinderella for hours before finally finding
her. The Fairy Godmother was thrilled that
the plan had worked.

"Well, I have some news of my own," said the Fairy Godmother excitedly. "I took your advice. I decided to start doing more interesting things."

As Verity looked around, she was surprised to see how clean and tidy the whole house looked.

The Fairy Godmother proudly showed Verity her kitchen shelves. They were full of glass jars with handwritten labels on the back of each one.

Verity picked up a jar and read the label. "Pickled Pumpkins!"

"That's right, dear," said the Fairy Godmother excitedly. "You say it all the time, so I thought—that's a good idea. Help yourself to as many jars as you like."

Verity didn't know what to say. She'd never tried eating pickled pumpkins before.

"Um, thank you," Verity said kindly. "Do you know what else is a good hobby?"

"What's that dear?" asked the Fairy Godmother.

"Making marshmallows," Verity said **knowingly**. "I can definitely help you eat those!"

*

A few weeks later, all the fairies gathered around the enchanted tree. They waited eagerly for Tatiana to present a sparkly star

---

knowingly   Deliberately and with awareness

to a lucky fairy. The silvery light of the full moon shone through the leaves.

Tatiana arrived in her long golden cloak, which matched her long golden hair. In her hands she held a large magical box. "This beautiful star is awarded to the fairy who has worked the hardest. Verity, this star is for you."

Everyone cheered as Verity stepped forward.

"Well done," said Tatiana proudly. "You learned that asking for help is more important than worrying about what others think of you."

Verity opened the box handed to her by Tatiana. She crossed her fingers and held her breath—she really wanted a lilac star. A beautiful sparkly jade-green star floated high into the sky and then landed in Verity's hands.

It was such a dazzling color that Verity wasn't disappointed.

"Thank you," she said happily.

Tatiana handed Verity another box. "This is a special gift for you from Cinderella."

Verity carefully opened the lid. Nestled inside was a pair of rainbow-colored slippers. She pulled off one of her sparkly purple boots and tried a slipper on.

"It fits! It fits!" Verity squealed with delight. "I'm going to wear these all the time—even to bed!" she said proudly.

Celeste giggled. "You're one of a kind, Verity!"

Fairy Quiz

1 Why were all the fairies gathered around the clock tower late at night?

2 What did Verity wish for when she blew out her candle?

3 What time did Cinderella have to be at the ball by?

4 What was the Fairy Godmother doing when Verity arrived at her house?

5 How many stepsisters does Cinderella have?

6 What did Cinderella drop as she ran away from the castle?

7 What was in the Fairy Godmother's glass jars in her kitchen?

8 What present did Cinderella give Verity at the end?

Answers

1. To celebrate the longest day of the year
2. Marshmallows 3. Eight thirty (8:30pm)
4. Watching TV 5. Two 6. Her glass slipper
7. Pickled pumpkins 8. Rainbow-colored slippers

Penguin Random House

Written by Caroline Wakeman
Illustrated by Amy Zhing
Designed by Collaborate Agency
Fiction Editor Heather Featherstone
Educational Consultants Jacqueline Harris, Jenny Lane-Smith
Senior Editors Amy Braddon, Marie Greenwood
US Senior Editor Shannon Beatty
Senior Designer Ann Cannings
Managing Editor Laura Gilbert
Managing Art Editor Diane Peyton Jones
Production Editor Rob Dunn
Production Controller Francesca Sturiale
Publishing Manager Francesca Young
verityfairy.com

First American Edition, 2021
Published in the United States by DK Publishing

1450 Broadway, Suite 801, New York, New York 10018
Copyright © 2021 Dorling Kindersley Limited
DK, a Division of Penguin Random House LLC

21 22 23 24 25 26 10 9 8 7 6 5 4 3 2 1
001–323743–Sep/2021

A catalog record for this book is available from the Library of Congress.
ISBN: 978-0-7440-3937-5 (Paperback)
ISBN: 978-0-7440-3938-2 (Hardcover)

DK books are available at special discounts when purchased in bulk for sales
promotions, premiums, fund-raising, or educational use. For details, contact:
DK Publishing Special Markets, 1450 Broadway, Suite 801,
New York, New York 10018
SpecialSales@dk.com

Printed and bound in Great Britain by
Clays Ltd, Elcograf S.p.A.

For the curious
www.dk.com

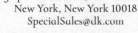